MARC BROWN

ARTHUR'S
FAMILY TREASURY

Three Arthur Adventures in One Volume

Little, Brown and Company

Boston   New York   London

1837

For my family with much love

First Edition

Arthur® is a registered trademark of Marc Brown.

Little, Brown originally published *Arthur's Birthday* (1989), *Arthur's Family
Vacation* (1993), and *Arthur's Baby* (1987) as individual picture books.

Library of Congress Cataloging-in-Publication Data

Brown, Marc Tolon.
   The Arthur family treasury / Marc Brown. — 1st ed.
   p.   cm.
   Contents: Arthur's birthday — Arthur's family vacation — Arthur's baby.
   ISBN 0-316-12147-9 (hc)
   1. Children's stories, American. [1. Aardvark Fiction.] I. Title.
PZ7.B81618A1dg 2000
[E] — DC21   99-26215

10 9 8 7 6 5 4 3 2 1

WOR

Printed in the United States of America

George Rizer, Boston Globe

The best thing a work of art can ever accomplish is to show or tell a story which helps us better understand who we are and how our community lives.

In almost every neighborhood — from the beginning of time — we can find an Arthur, a D.W., their friends, and (hopefully) a Grandma Thora.

Marc Brown's genius helps readers build common unity in a sometimes fragmented world: different people — and yet so much alike — all doing their best to live together in peace.

— FRED M. ROGERS, creator and
host of *Mister Rogers' Neighborhood*

Contents

Arthur's Birthday

Arthur's Family Vacation

Arthur's Baby

ARTHUR'S BIRTHDAY

"I can't wait! I can't wait!" said Arthur. "Are you sure it's only Tuesday?"
"See for yourself," said Mother.

"Four more days until my birthday!" said Arthur.
"I hope everyone can come to my birthday party."
"What kind of cake should I bake?" asked Grandma Thora.

"Chocolate!" said Arthur.

"Have a good day at school," said Mother, smiling.

"And don't forget to hand out your invitations," said D.W.

"Buster, can you come to my party?" asked Arthur.
"Are you kidding?" said Buster. "Of course!"
"Grandma's making chocolate cake," said Arthur.
"I'll be there!" said the Brain. "I love chocolate."

"How about me?" asked Binky Barnes.
"You're invited," said Arthur, "and Francine, too."
"Oh, boy," said Francine, "we can play spin the bottle!"

"Muffy, can you come to my birthday party?"
Arthur asked.
"Sure," Muffy answered. "When is it?"
"Saturday afternoon," Arthur said. "I can't wait."

"*This* Saturday afternoon? But that's when I'm having my party!" said Muffy.

"Oh, no!" said Arthur. "You can't. Can't you change your party to another day?"

"Are you kidding?" said Muffy. "The rock band and Pickles the Clown have been booked for months."

"I can't change my party, either," said Arthur. "All my relatives are coming from Ohio."

No one knew what to do.
Should they go to Arthur's
birthday party?

Or Muffy's?

Wednesday before school, the boys had a meeting.
"I think we should stick together," said Buster.
"Me, too!" said Binky.
"Right!" said the Brain. "We're all going to
Arthur's party."
"But what about the girls?" asked Arthur.
"Who needs girls?" said Buster.

The girls met out at the playground during lunch.
"Anyone who doesn't come to my party can't be my friend," said Muffy.
"But it won't be as much fun without the boys," said Francine.
"Are you my friend or not?" asked Muffy.

Thursday after school, Arthur and his mother picked out decorations for the party.
Later, the delivery man brought a big box.
"Wow! This weighs a ton!" said D.W.

In the mail, there were three birthday cards for Arthur.
One was from Uncle Bud. When Arthur opened it,
three dollar bills fell out.
"Some people have all the luck!" said D.W.

On the way home from school Friday, Arthur ran to catch up with Francine.

"I wish you could come to my party," said Arthur.

"I promised Muffy," said Francine. "But I wish I could go to both. What's a party without boys?"

"Wait a minute!" said Arthur.
"I have an idea."

"That's great," said Francine. "I'll help."

25

They ran to Arthur's tree house.
Arthur found pencils, paper, and envelopes.
"Let me write them," said Francine. "It has to look like Muffy's handwriting."
"Okay," said Arthur, "but be sure there's one for all the girls."

That night Arthur told his parents about his plan.
Early the next morning, Arthur and Francine delivered
their notes: one to Prunella, one to Sue Ellen, and
one to Fern.

The last note they delivered was a special one.
"All done," said Arthur.
"See you later!" said Francine.

"I smell pancakes!" said Arthur when he got home.
"Your favorite," said Father.
"And maple syrup all the way from Ohio," said
Aunt Bonnie.
"Happy birthday!" said Cousin George.

"Time for birthday kisses," said Mother.
"And eight birthday hugs," said Grandma Thora.
"Don't forget a pinch to grow an inch!" said D.W.

PIN THE TAIL

Arthur stood by the window. It was almost noon.
"Someone's coming!" he cried.
It was Sue Ellen.

"What are you doing here?" asked Sue Ellen.

"What are you doing here?" asked Buster.

"It's a surprise for Muffy," said Francine, coming up behind them.

"It's a surprise for all of us!" said the Brain.

"Everyone find a place to hide," said Arthur.

"Muffy will be here any minute!"

"Shhhh!" whispered Buster. "Here she comes!"
Arthur opened the door.
"Hi, Arthur, I came to pick up my present,"
said Muffy.

"Surprise!" shouted everyone.
"Happy birthday, Muffy!" said Arthur.
"See, I told you your present is too big to carry."
"The rest of your party is on the way," said Francine.
"After all," said Arthur, "what's a birthday party
without all your friends!"

"This is the best birthday ever," said Muffy. "We should do this every year!"
"But next year at your house," said Arthur's mom.

"Time to open presents," said Francine. "I picked this one out especially for you. You have to promise me you'll use it right away."

"Sure," said Arthur. "I can't wait."

"Happy birthday, Arthur!"

ARTHUR'S FAMILY VACATION

It was Arthur's last day of school.
Mr. Ratburn gave the class a surprise spelling test.
All the other classes were having parties.
"Finally, the moment you've all been waiting for,"
said Mr. Ratburn. "Report cards and . . ."

SUMMER

CAMP

". . . school's out!"

Everyone cheered.

"I can't wait for baseball practice to start," said Francine.

"I'm taking a college computer course," the Brain announced.

"I'll really miss you at Camp Meadowcroak this year, Arthur," Buster said.

"I wish I didn't have to go on vacation with my family," said Arthur. "There'll be nothing to do and no one to do it with."

"You'll have D.W., " Buster said, smiling. "For a whole week."

"Don't remind me," said Arthur.

Arthur's family spent that night packing.

"I wish I could take my dollhouse," said D.W.

"I wish Buster could come," said Arthur.

"This is a *family* vacation," said Mother.

"All we need for fun is each other," said Father.

"Let's take my swing set," said D.W. "We can all use that."

"Well, we're all packed," Father said the next morning.
"Where's Arthur?"
"He's on the phone with Buster," said Mother.
"For the hundredth time," D.W. added.
"Before we leave," said Father, "does anyone need
to use the bathroom?"
"This is your last chance," said Mother.
"Don't look at me!" said D.W.

"On our way at last." Mother smiled. "A whole week of no cooking!"

"And no dishes," said Father.

"A whole week without my best friend in the whole wide world," moaned Arthur.

"Once you're at the beach, you'll feel better," Father said.

"Are we there yet?" asked D.W. "I have to go to the bathroom."

Arthur spent the rest of the trip thinking about how much fun Buster must be having at camp.

"We're here!" said Mother.

"Welcome to the Ocean View," said the manager.

"Where's the ocean?" asked Father.

"Just across the highway behind that shopping center."
The manager pointed. "But there's a pool right here."

"Well, I guess I'll go swimming," said Arthur.

"Me, too," said D.W. "Wait for me!"

"Let's see our room first," said Mother.

"You mean we all have to stay in this puny little room?" asked D.W.

"Don't worry," said Mother. "We'll only be sleeping here."

"If you want to swim," said Arthur, "hurry up and get your suit on."

"We have the whole pool to ourselves," said Arthur.
"It's a good thing, too," said D.W. "Our bathtub is
bigger than this!"

That night at dinner, everyone ordered lobster.
"Buster loves lobster!" said Arthur.
"*This* is lobster?" said D.W. "I want a hot dog."

"Can we go to the beach tomorrow?" Arthur asked.
"Good idea!" said Father. "I'm sure the rain will stop by then."

"No beach today!" D.W. announced the next morning.
"I had a dream about Buster," said Arthur.
"Why don't you write him a postcard?" Mother
suggested.
"Why don't we all write postcards?" said Father.
"But what do we write about?" said D.W. "We haven't
done anything yet!"

Dear Buster,
I bet you're
having fun at
camp.
I wish I were
there.
      Your best friend,
          Arthur

POST CARD
Buster
Camp Meadowcroak

PLACE STAMP HERE

Dear Grandma Thora,
You were smart
to stay home!
XXXoxoxo
Love,
D.W. xxx ooo xxo xxxo

POST CARD
Grandma Thora
47 Oakmont St.

PLACE STAMP HERE

"What do we do now?" said D.W. "This vacation is a disaster."
At camp there's always something fun to do, thought Arthur. Even on rainy days.
"That's it!" he said. "I'm taking us on a field trip."

"I never heard of a *cow* festival," D.W. said. "But at least it's more fun than our motel room."

"Say 'cheese,'" said Father.

"Let's hurry or we'll miss the milking contest," said Arthur.

For the next few days, it rained and rained, but Arthur didn't mind. He was too busy planning new places to go. He forgot all about missing Buster.

On Wednesday, they went to Gatorville.
"At least the alligators get to swim," said D.W.

Thursday was busy, too. After touring Flo's Fudge Factory, they all went on Jimmy's Jungle Cruise.

"I never realized there are so many fun things to do in the rain," said Father.

"I want to plan a field trip, too," said D.W. "To the movies."

But when they got there, D.W. was too scared to watch.
"I thought it was a movie about fish," she whispered.

Finally, on Friday, their last day, the sun came out.
"What a day!" said Father.
"Just glorious!" said Mother.
Even D.W. was having fun.

No one wanted to leave, but the next day, they packed up and headed home.

"We're almost there," said Mother.

"Phew!" said D.W. "I really have to go to the bathroom."

"Oh, boy," said Arthur, "I can't wait to see Buster."

As soon as they got home, the doorbell rang.

It was Buster.

"Camp was fun, but I missed you," he said to Arthur.

"How was your vacation? How did you and D.W. get along?"

"Great!" said Arthur. "Take a look."

"Wow!" said Buster. "You really did have a great time."

ARTHUR'S BABY

"We have a surprise for you," said Mother
and Father.
"Is it a bicycle?" asked Arthur.

"We're going to have a baby!" said Mother.

"Oooooo," squealed D.W. "I love babies!"

"A *baby*?" said Arthur.

"Yes, in about six months," said Father.

"Plenty of time for us all to get ready."

Arthur's friends had lots of advice.
"Better get some earplugs," said Binky Barnes,
"or you'll never sleep."

"Forget about playing after school," said Buster.
"You'll have to babysit."

"You'll have to change all those dirty diapers!"
said Muffy.

"And you'll probably start talking baby talk,"
said Francine. "Doo doo ga ga boo boo."

For the next few months, everywhere Arthur
looked there were babies—more and more babies.
"I think babies are taking over the world!"
said Arthur.

WAA WAA WAAAAAA!

"Don't look now," said Buster, "but you could be in for triple trouble."

One day after school, D.W. grabbed Arthur's arm.
"I will teach you how to diaper a baby," she said.
"Don't worry about diapers," said Mother.
"Come sit next to me. I want to show you something."

Arthur age 9 months

"Is that really me?" asked Arthur.
"Yes," said Mother. "You were such a cute baby."

Arthur age 1 year

D.W. age 2 months

"Look," said D.W. "This is me with Mommy and Daddy. Don't I look adorable?"

D.W. age 5 months

That Saturday morning, Mother took out her suitcase.
"Where are you going?" asked Arthur.
"The baby could come any day now," said Mother.
"I need to be ready for the hospital."
"Here," said D.W. "Something for you to look at while
you're there."

Sunday morning, Arthur and D.W. found
Grandma Thora fixing breakfast.
"You have a new sister!" she said.
"Yippee! Yippee! Yippee!" said D.W. "She'll be
just like me!"
"That's what I'm afraid of," said Arthur.

The next day, they went to the hospital to see the new baby.

"We named her Kate," said Father.

"I think she has your nose, Arthur."

"I think she has D.W.'s mouth," said Arthur.

95

On Tuesday, Mother and Father brought Kate home.
Everyone was acting like they'd never seen a baby before.
Every time the doorbell rang, more presents arrived.
"They're not for you, Arthur," said D.W. "They're for
the baby."

"Arthur, don't you want to try holding Kate?"
Mother asked.
"Can I have another turn first?" asked D.W.
"It's Arthur's turn," Mother said.
"I'd rather look," said Arthur.
"It's just as well," said D.W. "Arthur doesn't
know beans about babies."

A few days later, Mother needed some help.
"I have to go upstairs," she said. "Arthur, would you
watch Kate?"
"*Me?*" asked Arthur. "What do I do?"
"Don't worry," said D.W. "I'll take care of everything."

When the doorbell rang, D.W. answered the door. "Arthur can't play," she said. "He has to babysit. But you can come in and see my baby."

"Don't get too close, because you all have germs! And be quiet," D.W. said, "my baby is sleeping."

"Look!" said Francine. "She opened her eyes."
"Stand back," said D.W. "She wants her bottle."

Kate drank her bottle in a flash.

Then she began to cry.
"Everyone remain calm," said D.W.

D.W. gave Kate a kiss.
Kate cried louder.

D.W. bounced Kate.
Kate screamed.

"Arthur, quick! Do something!" D.W. said. "She's your baby, too."

"All of a sudden she's *my* baby," said Arthur.

"Why is she crying?" asked D.W.

"She's trying to tell you something," said Arthur.

"What?" asked D.W.

"Listen carefully," said Arthur.

"Burp!" said Kate.
"Is everything all right?" asked Mother.
"It is now," Arthur answered.